GREAT MOMENTS IN OLYMPIC HISTORY

Olympic Track and Field

Brian Belval

New York

Published in 2007 by The Rosen Publishing Group, Inc.
29 East 21st Street, New York, NY 10010

Copyright © 2007 by The Rosen Publishing Group, Inc.

First Edition

All rights reserved. No part of this book may be reproduced in any form without permission in writing from the publisher, except by a reviewer.

Library of Congress Cataloging-in-Publication Data

Belval, Brian.
Olympic track and field / Brian Belval.
p. cm. – (Great moments in Olympic history)
Includes bibliographical references.
ISBN-13: 9781-4042-0971-8
ISBN-10: 1-4042-0971-9 (library binding)
1. Track and field—Juvenile literature. 2. Track and field athletes—Juvenile literature. 3. Olympics—History—Juvenile literature. I. Title.
GV1060.55.B45 2007
796.42–dc22

2006028069

Manufactured in the United States of America

On the cover: Wilma Rudolph races to the finish line during the 1960 Summer Olympics in Rome, Italy.

CONTENTS

CHAPTER 1

The First Olympics

The Olympic Games originated in Greece about 2,800 years ago. They took place at Olympia, in a group of buildings that included temples, a stadium that seated as many as 60,000 spectators, and numerous other structures. The original games were part of a religious festival. They were staged in honor of Zeus, the chief god of the Greeks, who was worshipped for strength, courage, and justice. The games were held every 4 years until A.D. 392. The following year, the Roman emperor Theodosius I banned the celebrations because they honored gods other than the Christian god.

Track-and-field events were an important part of the ancient Olympics. The first Olympics had only one event, a race of approximately 200 meters. Other events such as the pentathlon—which consisted of the discus throw, javelin throw, long jump, sprinting, and wrestling—were added over time. The games also had separate running events, such as 200-meter and 400-meter races, and a long distance race of roughly 5 kilometers.

Pierre de Coubertin

Pierre de Coubertin (1863–1937) was an enthusiastic sportsman who believed that sports played a critical role in the health and development of young people. His love of sports inspired him to bring back the Olympics, which he conceived as a sports competition and an international gathering to promote peace and goodwill. He met resistance when he announced his plans at an assembly of French sports officials in 1892. However, he persisted. At the International Congress on Amateurism in 1894, he persuaded seventy-nine sports experts from nine countries to establish the International Olympic Committee (IOC). In 1896, his dream came true when the first games of the modern era were held in Athens, Greece.

Coubertin's reign as leader of the Olympic movement was not without disagreements. He firmly believed that the games were for men. There was very limited participation by women. It was no accident that in 1928, after Coubertin stepped down as president of the International Olympic Committee, women's track and field became part of Olympic events. Despite his belief that only men should compete, Coubertin showed great leadership as the founder of the modern Olympic movement. Without him, it is very likely that the great international event we call the Olympics would never have come to be.

Pierre de Coubertin, founder of the modern Olympics, was born in Paris, France, in 1863.

The Modern Olympics

In 1896, the Olympic Games returned to Greece. The father of the modern games was Pierre de Coubertin, a Frenchman who admired ancient Greek culture. To honor the Greek heritage of the games, it was decided that the first modern Olympics would be held in Athens, Greece, and a new track-and-field event, the marathon, would be added to the program.

Coubertin and the organizers of the 1896 Olympics based the marathon on Greek historical events and legends. It was designed to be one of the high points of the Olympics. It would begin in the town of Marathon, and the course would wind approximately 25 miles (40 km) to the Olympic Stadium in Athens.

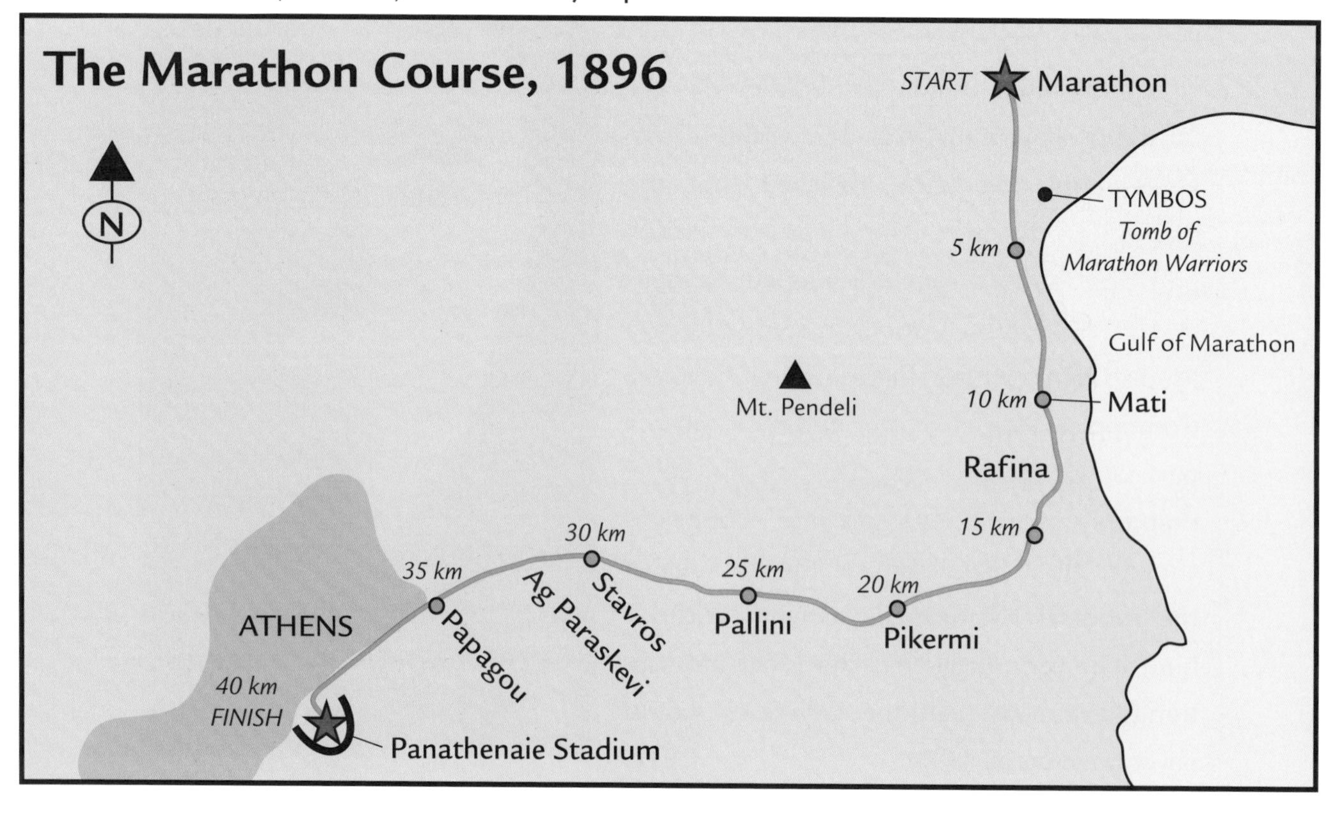

On the afternoon of April 10, 1896, seventeen runners gathered on the Marathon bridge for the start of the race. Among them were the top three finishers in the 1,500-meter race and Gyula Kellner, a talented long-distance runner from Hungary. The remaining thirteen competitors were from Greece.

Albin Lermusiaux of France, who had won the bronze medal in the 1,500-meter race, jumped out to an early lead. Halfway through the race, he had stretched his lead to 2 miles (3.2 km) ahead of the second-place runner, Edwin Flack of Australia. Arthur Blake of the United States was running third, and Kellner was fourth. All the Greek runners lagged behind.

After about 12.5 miles (20 km), Lermusiaux began to falter as he ran an uphill portion of the course. He was beginning to pay the price for his fast start. Flack passed him after about 19 miles (31 km), but Flack also struggled to maintain his pace. A number of Greek runners, who were more familiar with the course and accustomed to the heat, began to gain on Flack.

One of those runners was a 24-year-old shepherd from the village of Maroussi named Spyridon Louis. Louis had refreshed himself along the course with wine, milk, beer, orange juice, and a hard-boiled egg. Wearing shoes donated by his village, Louis caught up to Flack at about 21 miles (34 km), then slowly pulled ahead. About 100,000 spectators awaited the Greek hero at the Olympic Stadium. When he appeared at the marble entrance of

the stadium, the home crowd roared with delight. Two Greek princes ran with him to the finish line, then carried him in triumph to meet the king. The streets of Athens filled with fans as news of Louis's victory spread. He was showered with gifts and praise. His victory in the first Olympic marathon made Louis a Greek hero.

Spyridon Louis, winner of the marathon at the first modern Olympics, is shown wearing traditional Greek dress.

The Legend of Philippides

In 490 B.C., the Persian army landed at Marathon, a Greek port about 26 miles (42 km) from Athens. Upon learning of the approach of their enemies, the Athenians sent a messenger named Philippides to ask the Spartans for their help against the Persians. But instead of waiting for Sparta's aid, the Athenians launched a surprise attack against the Persians in Marathon. Although they were greatly outnumbered, the Athenians defeated the Persians. According to legend, a messenger was sent to take news of the victory to Athens. Upon arriving, he delivered the good news, collapsed, and died. Over the years, historians and writers combined these two stories into a single legend of Philippides: the brave young Greek messenger who rushed 26 miles (42 km) to announce the victory of the Athenian army at Marathon. This legend became the inspiration for the race created by Coubertin and his team.

This picture shows an artist's idea of what the scene might have looked like when Philippides collapsed after arriving in Athens.

The Events of Track and Field

In today's Olympic Games there are more than twenty track-and-field events. The track events involve running and hurdling; the field events involve throwing, jumping, and pole vaulting. Each event requires distinctive skills and training. Athletes must have immense devotion and commitment to be the best in the world. Some of the events we will read about include:

100-meter race: A prime event of the games, the winner is often named "the world's fastest" man or woman.

200-meter race: The 200-meter race requires the sprinters to run around a curved track rather than in a straight line, as they do in the 100-meter race.

javelin throw: The javelin is a spear that is tossed by a competitor after a short sprint. It may be made of metal or lightweight man-made material. The weight and length of the javelin differ in men's and women's competition.

high jump: In this event, the athlete leaps off one foot and then over a horizontal bar which is placed at increasingly greater heights.

long jump: A jump made from a running start to achieve the greatest distance.

hurdles: A race that involves running and jumping over

obstacles without breaking stride.

relay race: A race between teams in which each team member covers a certain part of the track. As each runner reaches the end of their section, they pass a baton to the next runner. This must occur within a specified area on the track.

Through the years, Olympic athletes have amazed the world with their feats. In this book, we will read about some historic Olympic athletes whose stories, like that of Spyridon Louis, are both impressive and inspiring. We will learn about a woman named Babe Didrikson, who became the first celebrity athlete in women's track and field. We will see how Jesse Owens achieved international fame when he won four Olympic gold medals. We will discover how courage and determination shaped Olympic athlete Wilma Rudolph. We will find out about the record-shattering leap of Olympian Bob Beamon. Reading accounts of amazing athletes such as these helps us to understand the drive for Olympic "gold"!

CHAPTER 2

Babe

Mildred "Babe" Didrikson was born on June 26, 1911, in Port Arthur, Texas. She was the sixth of seven children of Ole and Hannah Didriksen. According to one story, she got the nickname Babe because her family called her "Baby," which became "Babe" over time. Another story says she was nicknamed Babe because as a teenager she could hit home runs like famed baseball player Babe Ruth. She also changed the spelling of her last name from that of her parents by substituting an "o" for the "e."

Even at a young age, Babe was driven to become a world-class athlete. She once said, "I knew exactly what I wanted to be when I grew up. My goal was to be the greatest athlete who ever lived." The fiercely competitive Babe and her older sister, Lillie, were often seen racing each other and leaping over the hedges in the neighborhood. Babe even convinced her neighbors to trim the hedges so that they would all be of equal height, much like the hurdles in the track-and-field event.

Throughout her childhood, Babe loved to play sports, even those considered boy's sports, such as baseball. But that didn't bother Babe—she craved the competition and knew she could hold her own against the fastest and strongest boys in town.

After high school, Babe moved to Dallas, Texas, to play basketball for a team sponsored by the Employers Casualty Insurance Company. She was also hired to work at the company. She was paid $75 a month. The team, the Golden Cyclones, traveled throughout Texas competing against other company teams. They also competed in national tournaments sponsored by the Amateur Athletic Union (AAU). Babe flourished in her new setting. She was chosen as an All-American women's basketball player three times. In 1931, she led the Golden Cyclones to the national championship.

Babe is shown here as a member of the Brooklyn Yankees, a 1933 women's basketball team.

In 1930, the coach of the Golden Cyclones, Melvin J. McCombs, started training Babe in track and field. McCombs taught Babe the basics of the jumping, throwing, hurdling, and sprinting events. Soon, Babe became hooked. She trained tirelessly. Babe competed in the 1930 AAU national championships after

Women and the Olympics

Women's participation in the Olympics was a controversial topic in 1932. The founder of the modern Olympics, Pierre de Coubertin, did not believe that women should be included in the competition. He wanted the games to be like the original Greek Olympics, which were exclusively for men. Others believed that women taking part in sports, even outside the Olympic Games, was inappropriate. The ideal of the housewife who cared for the children and concentrated on household chores was very much alive in the 1920s and 1930s. Many believed a woman's place was at home, not on the competitive sports field. Sports were sometimes thought to bring out behaviors, such as aggression and competitiveness, that were not considered ladylike. Some were also concerned that intense physical exertion would harm a woman's body.

The International Olympic Committee finally agreed to add women's track and field to the Olympic program in 1928. Five events were chosen. In the 800-meter race, some competitors passed out from exhaustion at the finish line. A number of male sportswriters were distressed by the sight of female athletes pushing themselves to physical extremes. Their published accounts of the race renewed the argument over whether women should be allowed to compete in Olympic track and field. The IOC went back and forth over the issue but decided to keep the women's events in the games. In 1932, two more events were added: the 80-meter hurdles and the javelin throw. The 800-meter race, however, was dropped from the program and would not become a part of the games again until 1960.

only a few months of training and won four events. The Olympics were the following year, and Babe set her sights on multiple gold medals. It would be the first step in proving to the world that she was the greatest athlete who ever lived.

Babe's Quest for Gold

The 1932 AAU national championship, which doubled as the Olympic track-and-field trials, was held in Chicago, Illinois, in July. Babe was a one-woman team for Employers Casualty. Other teams had as many as twenty-five members, but Babe single-handedly captured the team championship. She won six events, three of which were Olympic events: the javelin throw, 80-meter hurdles, and high jump. Three days after the tryouts, Babe and others from the Olympic team boarded a train in Chicago's Union Station and headed for Los Angeles, California, the site of the 1932 Olympic Games.

When asked about her chances for winning the events she was entered in, Babe told reporters, "I am out to beat everybody in sight, and that's just what I'm going to do." Despite her strong beliefs in her abilities, the favorites in the javelin throw were actually two German throwers: Ellen Braumüller and Tilly Fleischer. Babe's first toss sailed 143 feet 4 inches (43.7 m), 10 feet (3 m) short of the world record but still an excellent throw. It was good enough for the gold medal. Babe beat Braumüller, whose best throw reached 142 feet 8 inches (43.5 m), and Fleischer, who finished third.

Babe Didrikson reaches back to throw the javelin during the 1932 Olympics in Los Angeles, California.

Babe's second event in her quest for triple gold was the 80-meter hurdles. In the qualifying heat, Babe broke the world record with a time of 11.8 seconds. In the finals, Babe lined up next to her main rival, Evelyne Hall, who finished second to Babe at the U.S. Olympic Trials. The runners dug in for the start before a large crowd. The crowd hushed in expectation of the race, then gasped as Babe burst off the starting block before the starting gun sounded. One more false start and she would be disqualified.

Babe played it safe for the restart and stayed down to be sure it didn't happen again. The slow start left her behind Evelyne Hall at the first hurdle. But Babe quickly made up ground. Babe raced evenly with Hall as they approached the last hurdle. At the finish line, they appeared to break the tape at the same time. The officials had to discuss the outcome of the race and reach an agreement on the result. After much deliberation, they announced Babe as the winner. The estimated margin of victory was only a few inches (cm). Both runners had been timed at 11.7 seconds, which was a new world record.

Babe's final event was the high jump, where she was expected to battle fellow American Jean Shiley for the gold medal. The two had tied for first place at the July trials. The large crowd followed the event closely. The tension mounted as one by one the jumpers were eliminated. Only Babe and Jean Shiley remained. Each jumped and cleared a world-record height of 5 feet 5 inches (1.65 m). But the

Jean Shiley uses the scissor style kick as she soars over the bar during her world record jump in the 1932 Los Angeles Olympic Games.

officials made a questionable decision. It was judged that Babe's final jump was illegal; she dove over the bar with her head before her feet, which at the time was against the rules. She was given the silver medal, while Jean Shiley won the gold.

Despite being disappointed about not winning a third gold medal, Babe had captured the hearts of the American public. She had become the first celebrity athlete in women's track and field. Babe's achievements and confident, competitive spirit inspired many young women to do as she had done: pick up a baseball, race against the boys, and enjoy the healthy competition offered by athletics.

A Great Achievement

The year was 1935. Berlin, Germany, had been chosen as the site for the Olympic Games that would be held the following year. However, religious leaders and politicians all over the world were calling for a boycott. They were opposed to the racist laws and policies that had been passed in Germany by Adolf Hitler and the Nazi party. In the United States, many people believed boycotting the Olympics would send a message to the Nazis that their beliefs were not acceptable. Others, however, believed that politics should not mix with sports. Athletes trained for many years. To see their dreams shattered because of politics seemed unfair. In the end, the U.S. Olympic Committee decided to send their team to Germany. The press in the United States dubbed the 1936 Olympics the "Nazi Games." Many athletes understood that they were competing against more than the clock or fellow opponents. They were also competing against a philosophy of hatred. Victory on the track or in the field would symbolize victory over prejudice.

A runner arrives in Berlin, Germany, carrying the Olympic torch. The modern torch relay was introduced at the Berlin games in 1936.

Out of Alabama

One athlete who competed in the 1936 Olympics was born on September 12, 1913, in Oakville, Alabama. James Cleveland "Jesse" Owens was born into a poor African American family. His father was a sharecropper, a type of farmer who receives his land and supplies from a landowner and pays him back with a portion of his crop. Sharecropping families lived from season to season. A bad harvest meant that food and supplies would be scarce during the winter months.

This 1935 photo was taken at a home in a sharecropper community in Arkansas.

In 1922, the Owens family moved to Cleveland, Ohio, in search of a better life. Jesse was not healthy as a young child. His mother cared for him at home because the family could not afford a doctor. Under his mother's care, Jesse grew stronger as he grew older.

In junior high school, Jesse met Charles Riley, who would become his coach and guiding force. Riley noticed Jesse's natural athletic ability and asked him to join the junior high track team. Since Jesse worked after school to help support his family, Riley convinced him to train in the morning before school. Riley taught Jesse proper method and training habits. He also taught him the mental aspects of the sport. Jesse's hard work soon paid off. In 1928, he set a world record for junior high athletes with a mark of 22 feet $11\frac{3}{4}$ inches (7 m) in the long jump.

In high school, Jesse dominated the competition. He capped off his senior year with a national high school record in the long jump of 24 feet 11$\frac{1}{4}$ inches (7.6 m).

Jesse Owens: Record-Breaker

Jesse continued his athletic career at Ohio State University. Ohio State is a member of the Big Ten Conference of college teams. At the Big Ten Championships in 1935, Jesse astounded the world with one of the most remarkable performances in track-and-field history. In less than an hour, Jesse set three world records and tied another. His long jump record of 26 feet 8$\frac{1}{4}$ inches (8.1 m) would last until 1960. In one afternoon, Jesse had gone from a promising track-and-field athlete to an American celebrity. As he traveled with his Ohio State team from meet to meet, he was swarmed by autograph seekers and reporters.

At the Olympic Trials in July 1936, Jesse won the 100-meter race, 200-meter race, and long jump. Jesse and his Olympic teammates boarded the SS *Manhattan* on July 15 with high expectations. Jesse was favored to win all three of his individual events; anything less than three gold medals would be a major disappointment. A 9-day trip across the Atlantic Ocean was followed by a short train ride to Berlin. There the athletes were paraded down streets that flew the Nazi flag toward the newly constructed Olympic Village. The athletes might have expected a cold reception from the German people, but that was not the case. German sport fans took their photographs. The athletes were cheered. People asked for their autographs. Just as in the United States, the German people idolized Jesse.

Olympic Feats of Courage and Determination

Over 100 years of the modern Olympic Games have provided countless world records, amazing races, and moments of glory for the victors. But the Olympics are about much more than simply winning. The Olympics showcase the athlete's will to endure, overcome difficulty, and persist against all odds. For many athletes, victory consists of simply making it to the finish line:

Pawel Januszewski (Poland): In 1997, this 400-meter hurdler was severely injured in a car accident. Amazingly, he recovered, and 9 months later, he won the 400-meter hurdles in the European Championships. In 2000, he placed sixth in the 400-meter hurdles at the Summer Olympics in Sydney, Australia.

Abdul Baser Wasigi (Afghanistan): As a child and young adult, Wasigi saw his country ruined by war. In spite of turmoil at home, he was determined to compete in the 1996 Olympics in Atlanta, Georgia. He would not let his dream be shattered even after injuring his leg 2 weeks before the games. Wasigi limped the 26 miles (42 km) of the marathon to finish in last place.

Derek Redmond (Great Britain): During the 400-meter semifinals in Barcelona, Spain, in 1992, Redmond tore a muscle in his leg less than halfway through the race. His father, seeing his son in severe pain, left his seat in the stands to help him. Men arrived with a stretcher to carry him off the track, but Redmond waved them away. In tears, he lifted himself up and began to limp on one leg. His father reached him with about 120 meters to go in the race. He put his arm around his son's waist, and with great effort, they moved down the track. Redmond's father let go of him just before the finish line, and Redmond completed the race on his own. The crowd of 65,000 stood and cheered as Redmond struggled across the finish line.

Four Gold Medals and a Friend for Life

The 100-meter finals took place on August 3. It was a cold, wet day. The track was not in the best shape. Jesse got off to a clean start, broke ahead of the field, and led the race the rest of the way. When Jesse's time of 10.3 seconds was announced, the crowd thundered with approval. He tied the world record, which was especially amazing considering the less-than-ideal running conditions.

Jesse had little time to celebrate, since the 200-meter qualifying heats and long jump qualifying and finals were being held the next day. To qualify for the long jump finals, Jesse needed to jump 23 feet 5 inches (7.1 m). He expected to qualify easily, since the qualifying distance was more than 3 feet (0.9 m) less than his best mark. Still wearing his warm-ups, Jesse raced down the runway for a practice jump. As he stepped over the take-off board, the official thrust a red flag into the air to signal that the jump was a foul. No one had told Jesse that practice jumps were not allowed. Jesse's practice jump was considered his first jump. Jesse prepared for his second jump, determined to qualify and then rest up for his next event. But on his next jump, he again fouled. Suddenly, Jesse felt an enormous amount of pressure. If he didn't reach the qualifying distance on his third and final jump, he would not be able to compete in the finals.

As Jesse prepared for what would be the most important jump of his career, he was approached by a German jumper named Lutz

Long. Long was several inches taller than Jesse, well muscled, blond, and blue eyed. Long set an Olympic record with his first qualifying jump. Jesse knew that Long would be his main competitor.

Lutz Long and Jesse Owens talk at Berlin Stadium during the 1936 Berlin Olympics.

According to stories Jesse told years later, Long was friendly to him. As Long talked to him, Jesse began to feel some of the pressure lessen. Long suggested that Jesse mark a spot about 6 inches (15.2 cm) behind the take-off board and aim for that. This would help make sure that he didn't foul again. Jesse saw the wisdom of Long's advice and followed it. He qualified easily with a jump of more than 25 feet (7.6 m).

During the finals, Long and Jesse squared off against each other. Jesse jumped 25 feet $10\frac{1}{2}$ inches (7.9 m). This was an Olympic record. Long then fired up the German crowd with a jump of the same length. On his final jump, Jesse soared to 26 feet $5\frac{1}{2}$ inches (8.1 m). With Adolf Hitler in the stadium as a witness, Long rushed up to congratulate Jesse on his amazing performance.

Long's display of sportsmanship contrasted with the hateful beliefs of Hitler and the Nazis. The cheers of the crowd greeted Owens as he stood on the medal stand and showed that much of Germany saw the world very differently from the way its leaders did.

Jesse would add two more gold medals to his collection in the games: the 200-meter race and the 4x100-meter relay. He would also become close friends with Lutz Long. The two were often seen together in the Olympic Village and continued to exchange letters after the Olympic Games ended and Jesse returned home.

Jesse Owens sails through the air during the 1936 Olympic long jump competition.

CHAPTER 4

Wilma Rudolph: A Graceful Champion

Wilma Rudolph was born on June 23, 1940, into a large family. She was the twentieth of twenty-two children. She was born sooner than she was supposed to be and weighed only about 4.5 pounds (2 kg) at birth.

Wilma was small and sickly as a young child. At the age of 4, she came down with polio, which left her unable to use her left leg. Twice a week, her mother would drive her 45 miles (72 km) from their home in Clarksville, Tennessee, to Nashville for treatment. Wilma wore a brace and a special shoe that allowed her to limp slowly from place to place. By age 12, she was finally able to walk normally again.

Wilma's first love was basketball. Once she had regained the use of her leg, she spent much of her free time playing basketball or watching others play. Wilma made it onto her junior high basketball team. However, she was not one of the top players, and it was 3 years before she played a single game. In high school, however, she became a star player. Her coach nicknamed her "Skeeter" (another name for mosquito) because she was quick, skinny, and always in his way.

A Natural Talent

Soon, it became clear that Wilma had another talent besides basketball. The basketball coach, Clinton Gray, wanted to put together a track-and-field team at the school. He asked Wilma to join the team. Her natural ability became apparent almost immediately. Wilma was the fastest runner on the team and won races with ease.

By her second year in high school, Wilma had grown to 5 feet 11 inches (1.8 m). She was the top track athlete at her school and had also blossomed into its best basketball player. The leg brace and special shoe were a distant memory.

That same year, she met Ed Temple, the coach of the Tennessee State University (TSU) women's track-and-field team. He saw Wilma at a track-and-field event and invited her to begin training at the women's summer track program at TSU. Temple quickly realized Wilma's potential and instructed her closely on proper form and breathing techniques. He also worked on her starts and

Wilma Rudolph catches her breath after setting a world record of 11.3 seconds in the 100-meter race at the 1961 USA-USSR track meet in Moscow.

taught her how to use starting blocks. At the end of the summer, Temple took Wilma to the Amateur Athletic Union national track meet in Philadelphia, Pennsylvania, where she won all nine events she had entered.

Shortly after the start of her junior year in high school, Wilma joined Temple and his Tennessee State team at the Olympic track-and-field trials in Seattle, Washington. Wilma was only 16 years old and would be racing against athletes many years older. Despite her inexperience, she made the Olympic team in the 200-meter race and the 4x100-meter relay. The 1956 games, which were held in Melbourne, Australia, were somewhat of a disappointment for Wilma. She failed to reach the finals in the 200-meter race, and the relay team took the bronze medal. Any other 16-year-old would have been overjoyed to earn an Olympic medal, but not Wilma. She would settle for nothing less than gold. Four years later, Wilma would have the chance to capture gold not once, but three times.

Ed Temple and the Tigerbelles

Women's track and field in the 1960s was dominated by the women of Tennessee State University. The coach of the team, Ed Temple, took over the Tennessee State program in 1953 and promptly named the team the Tigerbelles. Under Temple's leadership, the Tigerbelles won twenty-three Olympic medals, thirteen of which were gold. In addition to Wilma Rudolph, Olympic legend Wyomia Tyus also trained under Temple's watchful eye. Tyus won gold medals in the 1964 and 1968 games in the 100-meter race, becoming the first sprinter, male or female, to win consecutive gold medals in the race.

Left to right are members of the TSU women's track-and-field team, the Tigerbelles: Martha Hudson, Lucinda Williams, Wilma Rudolph, and Barbara Jones.

The 1960 Games

The 1960 Olympic Games were held in Rome, Italy. Wilma qualified for three events: the 100-meter race, 200-meter race, and the 4x100-meter relay. The relay team consisted of Wilma and three teammates from Tennessee State. Wilma dominated the 100-meter race, winning the final by 3 meters (9.8 ft). Wilma also dominated the 200-meter race. She won the final in 24 seconds. Even though she won, Wilma was disappointed that she had run slower than her world record of 22.9 seconds. There was some consolation in her performance in the semifinals, where she had set an Olympic record of 23.2 seconds.

The relay was scheduled for September 11, 1960, the final day of the games. A huge crowd anxiously awaited the start of the race. All over the world, sports fans gathered around their televisions. The 1960 Olympics were the first games to be fully covered by television, and Wilma had captured the hearts of viewers worldwide.

After the first three legs of the race, the U.S. team led by about 2 meters. Wilma had been chosen to run the final leg. She waited for the baton from her teammate, Lucinda Williams, while the crowd roared with excitement. As Wilma reached back to receive the baton, it almost fell to the ground. She slowed down for a split second to make sure she had it firmly in her grasp. This cost the American team their lead. As Wilma raced around the final

Wilma Rudolph, nicknamed the "black gazelle" because of her long, graceful stride, crosses the finish line in the 1960 Olympic 100-meter race.

turn, the U.S. team had dropped to second place.

Wilma reached deep inside for all she had. She was determined not to let her teammates down. She passed the German runner ahead of her and took the lead. As Wilma broke the tape in first place, she was overwhelmed with happiness. She had become the first U.S. woman to win three gold medals in a single Olympics. Best of all, she was able to celebrate the achievement with her teammates and friends from Tennessee State University.

CHAPTER 5

A Record-Shattering Leap

Bob Beamon was born on August 29, 1946. He grew up on the streets of South Jamaica, a poor neighborhood in New York City. He had a difficult childhood. His mother died when he was just a baby. He never knew his father. He was raised by his grandmother. Although she did her best to care for him, she struggled to make ends meet. Bob often skipped class because he preferred life on the street over school. At age 14, he was thrown out of school because of his behavior. He was sent to a school for boys with problems. The school was a wake-up call for Bob. He knew he had to turn his life around.

Athletics helped Bob put his past behind him. As a teenager, he competed in the Junior Olympics, a sports program of qualifying meets and final competitions for young athletes. Bob broke the Junior Olympic long jump record with a leap of 24 feet (7.3 m). His athletic success inspired him to become more focused at school. He soon left the school for students with behavior problems and enrolled at Jamaica High School, one of the top academic schools in the city. With the help of Jamaica's coach, Bob continued to improve his jumping and received an athletic scholarship to the University of Texas at El Paso.

Bob Beamon sails through the air during a long jump at the 1968 Olympics in Mexico City, Mexico.

The Qualifying Round

In 1968, the Olympics were being held in Mexico City. Bob, at the age of 22, was a member of the U.S. team. Bob had received a scare on the day of qualifying for the Olympic finals. Competitors had to jump over 27 feet (8.2 m) to qualify. Bob was nervous and unable to focus when he reached the stadium. He fouled on his first two qualifying jumps; he had only one jump left. As he prepared for his third and final jump, Ralph Boston, his teammate and a world-record holder, came up to him. Ralph reminded Bob that Jesse Owens had been in a similar situation in the 1936 Olympics. He told Bob to aim for a spot well behind the take-off board so that he didn't foul. Bob listened to Boston and qualified easily.

The Final

On the day of the finals, Bob arrived at the stadium much more relaxed than the day before. He felt confident that he had a big jump in him. When it was Bob's turn, he found his mark and prepared for his jump. His nineteenth and final stride was timed perfectly. He lifted off and rose into the air of the Estadio Olímpico Universitario. Witnesses estimate that Bob rose to a height almost 6 feet (1.8 m) above the pit, which was unusually high for the event. His long arms were stretched out for balance, somewhat like airplane wings. His knees were tucked into his chest. When Bob came down, the force of the landing made him bounce up

Modification of the Long Jump

The long jump is an event in which athletes jump as far as possible from a running start. The long jump was an event in the original Olympic Games of ancient Greece. The Greeks jumped from a standing position. They also used weights that were held in their hands. These weights, known as halteres, were made of stone or lead. The athletes would hold a haltere in each hand. When they were ready to jump, they would swing their weighted arms forward. When they were about to land, they would swing their weighted arms behind their body. The weights, swinging forward at the beginning of the jump, were thought to help the jumper move forward and upward. Swinging the weights behind the body upon landing was thought to help the jumper position his feet farther out, thus gaining greater distance.

and out of the pit. Bob sensed that he had unleashed a good jump, perhaps a world record, but he wasn't sure. The crowd roared, while Bob stood and anxiously awaited the result.

The officials were using a state-of-the-art device to measure the jumps. It ran on a rail beside the pit and detected the impression left in the sand by the jumper. However, when the officials moved the device toward the mark left by Bob's jump, it slid off the rail. The system's designers had not expected a leap longer than the world record of 27 feet $4\frac{3}{4}$ inches (8.4 m). Many minutes passed while officials located a measuring tape. They measured and remeasured the jump, shocked by the length and wanting to double-check that the measurement was correct. The result finally flashed on the scoreboard: 8.9 m (29 feet $2\frac{1}{2}$ inches). Bob did not react immediately because he was unfamiliar with the metric system. Then the measurement was converted into feet and Bob learned that he had broken 29 feet! A Soviet jumper, Igor Ter-Ovanesyan, turned to the other competitors and said, "Compared to this jump, we are as children."

Bob had set a new Olympic record. In an instant, he had also shattered the world record by nearly 2 feet (.6 m). To put this record into perspective, consider that in the 33 years prior to Bob's jump, the world long jump record had only increased $8\frac{1}{2}$ inches (21.6 cm). Bob Beamon added $21\frac{3}{4}$ inches (55.2 cm) to the existing world record. He had shattered not only the world record but also his own personal best. His record lasted almost 23 years. In 1991, American Mike Powell jumped 29 feet $4\frac{1}{2}$ inches (9 m) to set a new world record. However, to this day, many consider the jump by Bob Beamon the greatest feat in Olympic history.

The Future of Olympic Track and Field

More than 100 years of Olympic history have shown us amazing athletic feats, memorable acts of courage, and unforgettable moments of grace and glory. In this book, we have looked at some of the great and inspiring moments in the history of Olympic track and field.

Today, we watch and read about a new generation of track-and-field athletes. Sprinters Veronica Campbell of Jamaica and Justin Gatlin of the United States, marathon runners Mizuki

Bob Beamon makes his record-breaking jump of 29 feet $2\frac{1}{2}$ inches (8.9 m) at the 1968 Olympics in Mexico City.

Bob Beamon is overcome with emotion after setting a new world record in the 1968 Olympic long jump. His record stood for more than 22 years.

Noguchi of Japan and Stefano Baldini of Italy, and hurdler Liu Xiang of China all won gold medals at the 2004 Olympic Games in Athens, Greece. They are just a few of the rising stars in track and field. As events of future Olympic Games are contested, we can watch pole vaulters soar to new heights, we can marvel at the speed and power of the world's fastest runners, and we can feel the anticipation as athletes strive for their dreams.

One goal of Olympic athletes is to win and prove to the world that they are the best in their sport. But the Olympic Games are also about personal victories. As we have seen, Olympic athletes are a source of astonishing stories and images. They teach us what determination and belief in a dream can achieve.

Timeline

776 B.C. First recorded ancient Olympics in Greece.

April 10, 1896: Athens, Greece: Spyridon Louis of Greece wins the gold medal in the first Olympic marathon.

July 31, 1932: Los Angeles, California: Babe Didrikson captures the gold medal in the javelin throw.

August 4, 1932: Los Angeles, California: Didrikson wins the gold medal in the 80-meter hurdles in world-record time.

August 7, 1932: Los Angeles, California: Didrikson claims the silver medal in the high jump.

August 3, 1936: Jesse Owens sprints to victory in Berlin in the 100-meter race.

August 4, 1936: Berlin, Germany: Owens defeats Lutz Long for the gold medal in the long jump final.

August 5, 1936: Berlin, Germany: Owens wins the gold medal in the 200-meter race.

August 9, 1936: Owens wins his fourth gold medal of the Berlin games as a member of the 4x100-meter relay team.

December 1956: Melbourne, Australia: Wilma Rudolph earns a bronze medal as a member of the 4x100-meter relay team.

September 2, 1960: Wilma Rudolph captures her first gold medal in the 100-meter race in Rome.

September 1960: Rome, Italy: Rudolph wins another gold medal in the 200-meter race.

September 11, 1960: Rome, Italy: Rudolph and her teammates from Tennessee State University win the gold medal in the 4x100-meter relay.

October 18, 1968: Mexico City, Mexico: Bob Beamon soars to a new world record in the long jump for his first and only gold medal.

August 30, 1991: Tokyo, Japan: Mike Powell establishes a new world record in the long jump.

August 13–29, 2004: Summer Olympics held in Athens, Greece.

August 8–24, 2008: Summer Olympics held in Beijing, China.

Glossary

baton A short metal tube passed from one runner on a relay team to the next during a race.

boycott A refusal to do business or engage in friendly activities with an individual, company, or nation in an effort to punish or show objection to something.

heat In track and field, an early race in which only the top finishers advance to the next round.

heritage Something one receives as a result of birth or one's natural situation.

hurdle A light, movable obstacle that competitors must jump over while racing.

Nazi A member of the political party that controlled Germany from 1933–1945.

outnumber To exceed in number.

Persian A person from the country Persia (modern-day Iran), which is located in southwest Asia.

pit The rectangular area filled with sand that serves as the landing area for the long jump competition.

pole vault An event in which competitors leap over a very high bar with the help of a long pole.

polio A disease that causes muscle weakness and sometimes leaves a person unable to move.

politician A person actively involved in conducting the business of a government.

potential Something that can develop.

racist Relating to the mistaken belief that one race of people is better than another.

semifinals Next-to-last elimination in a competition.

sprinter Someone who races at top speed, especially for short distances.

starting block A sloping device that a runner puts their feet against and pushes off from at the start of a race.

take-off board The board at the end of the runway for the long jump. Competitors must jump from behind the board.

For More Information

International Association of Athletics Federations
17 rue Princesse Florestine
Monte-Carlo
98007 Monaco Cedex
Tel: 377-93-10-88-88
http://www.iaaf.org

International Olympic Committee
Château de Vidy
1007 Lausanne
Switzerland
Tel: 41-21-621-61-11
http://www.olympic.org

U.S. Olympic Training Center–Colorado Springs
National Headquarters
1 Olympic Plaza
Colorado Springs, CO 80909
(719) 632-5551
http://www.usoc.org

USA Track & Field
1 RCA Dome, Suite 140
Indianapolis, IN 46225
(317) 261-0500
http://www.usatf.org

Web Sites

Due to the changing nature of Internet links, the Rosen Publishing Group, Inc., has developed an online list of Web sites related to the subject of this book. This site is updated regularly. Please use this link to access the list: **http://www.rosenlinks.com/gmoh/trac**

For Further Reading

Anderson, Dave. *The Story of the Olympics.* New York: HarperCollins Publishers, 2000.

Cayleff, Susan E. *Babe Didrikson: The Greatest All-Sport Athlete of All Time.* Newburyport, MA: Conari Press, 2000.

Fisher, David. *The Encyclopedia of the Summer Olympics.* London: Franklin Watts, 2003.

Gifford, Clive. *Summer Olympics: The Definitive Guide to the World's Greatest Sports Celebration.* Boston, MA: Kingfisher, 2004.

Macy, Sue. *Swifter, Higher, Stronger: A Photographic History of the Summer Olympics.* Washington, DC: National Geographic Children's Books, 2004.

Raatma, Lucia. *Jesse Owens: Track-and-Field Olympian.* Chanhassen, MN: Child's World, 2003.

Rennert, Rick. *Jesse Owens: Champion Athlete.* Minneapolis, MN: Sagebrush, 2001.

Ruth, Amy. *Wilma Rudolph.* Minneapolis, MN: Lerner Publishing Co., 2000.

Schraff, Anne E. *Wilma Rudolph: The Greatest Woman Sprinter in History.* Berkeley Heights, NJ: Enslow Publishers, 2004.

Wakeman, Nancy. *Babe Didrikson Zacharias: Driven to Win.* Minneapolis, MN: Lerner Publishing Co., 2000.

Bibliography

Ashe, Arthur R., Jr. *A Hard Road to Glory–Track and Field: The African American Athlete in Track and Field.* New York: Amistad, 1993.

Baker, William J. *Jesse Owens: An American Life.* New York: The Free Press, 1986.

Beamon, Bob, and Milana Walter Beamon. *The Man Who Could Fly: The Bob Beamon Story.* Columbus, MS: Genesis Press, 1999.

Cayleff, Susan A. *Babe: The Life and Legend of Babe Didrikson Zacharias.* Champaign, IL: University of Illinois Press, 1995.

Guttmann, Allen. *The Olympics: A History of the Modern Games.* Champaign, IL: University of Illinois Press, 2002.

Lovett, Charlie. *Olympic Marathon: A Centennial History of the Games' Most Storied Race.* Westport, CT: Praeger Publishers, 1997.

Owens, Jesse, with Paul Neimark. *Jesse: The Man Who Outran Hitler.* New York: Fawcett, 1978.

Pieroth, Doris H. *Their Day in the Sun: Women of the 1932 Olympics.* Seattle, WA: University of Washington Press, 1996.

Schaap, Dick. *The Perfect Jump.* New York: Signet, 1976.

Wallechinsky, David. *The Complete Book of the Summer Olympics.* Toronto, Canada: SportClassic Books, 2004.

Index

About the Author

Brian Belval is a sports aficionado and former track-and-field athlete. In 1990, he was a member of the Illinois state champion 4x800-meter relay team. He has since moved to New York City, where he works as an editor.

Photo Credits

Cover © Jerry Cooke/Corbis; pp. 5, 13 © Bettmann/Corbis; pp. 8, 9, 16, 18, 21, 27, 30, 32 © Getty Images; p. 22 © Corbis; pp. 26, 34, 37 © AFP/Getty Images; p. 41 © Tony Duff/Allsport; p. 42 © Time & Life Pictures/Getty Images.

Designer: Michael J. Flynn
Editor: Mary Ann Hoffman

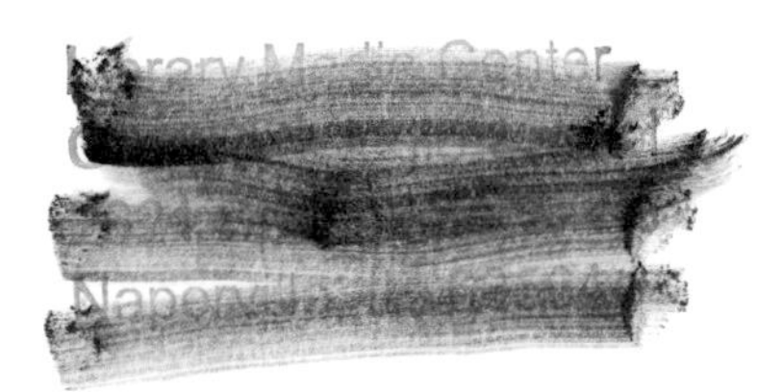